Charlotte
Learns to Write

Written by Kathryn Sherry

Illustrated by Cristal Baldwin

For Tessa -
keep reading
& dream
big!
♡
Kathryn Sherry

CHARLOTTE LEARNS TO WRITE

First Old Scout Press Edition June 2018

Old Scout Press
Charlotte, NC

www.OldScoutPressCharlotte.com

ISBN: 978-0692119020

Book design by Meredith Ray

1   3   5   7   9   10   8   6   4   2

For my parents,
who always nurtured my love of stories
and inspired my imagination to grow...

...even when that vivid imagination lead to
inking a fantastical world on the hallway wallpaper.

Charlotte has always loved to read...

...then she went to kindergarten and learned how to write.

Charlotte loves to write.

Loves to write.

She writes with chalk
on the driveway
while her big brother,
Bradford, shoots
hoops.

But then the rain comes and washes away her words.

She writes on the white tiles using washable markers during bathtime.

But the bubbles and bathwater
make her sentences streak.

Soon the water and Charlotte
are rainbow colors.

She writes on the walls using her pink sparkly crayon.

But Charlotte's mom does not like that idea.

Charlotte's dad is
always reading
"The Paper."

So, Charlotte
writes on the
newspaper.

But Charlotte's dad has not read it yet.

Today as Charlotte's dad picks her up from school he says, "Charlotte, I have a surprise for you at home."

Charlotte beams with excitement. She thinks about all of the surprises her favorite storybook characters have had.

The surprise could be a pet elephant.

Maybe her parents built a runway in the yard and they are going to jet off to Paris!

The surprise could be that the circus has come to town and they need a new Ring Leader.

Naturally, Charlotte would be the right fit for the job.

Or perhaps Charlotte's dad created a time machine.

Traveling back in time would certainly help Charlotte with her school project on dinosaurs!

When Charlotte and her dad arrive home, Charlotte skips inside the house, ready for her big surprise.

Her dad hands her a wrapped present.

Charlotte yanks off the bow and tears open the pretty wrapping paper.

Inside she finds sheets of paper with
Charlotte's Stories written at the top.

Her own stationary to write poetry,
fairytales, and soliloquies on!

The most
wonderful gift
of all!

Charlotte hugs her dad and runs to her room where she writes and writes until her hand gets tired.

Charlotte puts her crayon down.

She cuddles up on her special chair
with her dog, Boo Boo, and reads a book.

Charlotte loves to write, but reading is still her favorite.

About the Author

Connecticut native, Kathryn Sherry, resides in Charlotte, NC. While the main character's moniker is influenced by the city she considers home, the character of Charlotte is inspired by Kathryn's childhood love of books and memories of her father reading her favorite stories two, sometimes three, times every night. Despite the oversized bows her mother would perch on her head as a child, Kathryn managed to peer out and read, taking that passion to Lynchburg College where she earned a Bachelor of Arts in English with an emphasis in Creative Writing. Her passion for children's literature and writing led to working in publishing in New York and later a return to school to obtain a Masters in Elementary Education. Now in her eighth year of teaching, Kathryn nurtures her kindergarten students' imagination and love of reading every day.

About the Illustrator

Cristal Baldwin is an artist that lives in the small town of London, Ohio. She resides there with her husband, son, a rescue dog, kitty and another rescue cat. They like to sit on her artwork when she is not looking. Cristal received her fine arts degree from Wittenberg University, in Springfield, Ohio, and continues to create a variety of artwork.

www.flyingfrogstudio.net

Made in the USA
Lexington, KY
09 June 2018